The Kingdom Leader in You

What to Know as You Grow

Dr. Apostle Daniel F. Andrews

For permission requests, write to the author, addressed to:

Dr. Apostle Daniel F. Andrews

To my wife and children, thank you for your unwavering support and sacrificial love. To every mentor, friend, and fellow laborer who has poured into my life, you are woven into every word. This work reflects your investment, and I honor you.

Let us lead not for applause, but for impact. Not for recognition, but for transformation. And above all, let us lead as Christ led with a towel in hand and love in our hearts.

Endorsements

"This book will prove to be resourceful, to equip Leaders in Ministry and Business.

Let it serve as a guide to help you avoid the failures that could hinder your success. Apostle Dr Daniel Andrews, Overseer of A.I.M. Is experienced and anointed for the end times. He is exposing the schemes of darkness that have the same motives, just in a different time. Also, the Leadership Character, Practical Application, and Reflection questions will train and teach you to be prepared for these encounters."

Prophetess Gina L. Pimentel Spease,
Overseer of Grace Tabernacle, Pottstown, Pa 19464

"What to Know as You Grow Knowing Your Calling, Face Your Battles & Lead with Purpose. There is a stark difference in leading people from position versus leading people from the heart of God. Dr. Daniel Andrews shares wisdom gained from his personal experience and presents his readers with the necessary strategies, while equipping and empowering them to be overcomers. This book is a must-read and a powerful resource that will transform your perception of leadership!"

Pastor Shawn Adam Hoffmaster
Pastor of Providence Place Senior Living

"I have had the honor of traveling the world and ministering alongside Apostle Dr. Daniel Andrews, and I can say without hesitation he is the real thing. *The Kingdom Leader in You* is not theory; its revelation lived and proven through years of faithful service. Dr. Andrews writes with the heart of a spiritual father and the wisdom of a seasoned leader. Every page will stir your spirit, challenge your mindset, and equip you to lead with courage, humility, and divine purpose."

Apostle Dr. Brian Alton

Presiding Bishop, I.C.A.L.M. International Covering Alliance & Licensing for Ministries Founder, Chancellor, Gateway International Bible Institute

Founder, Apostle, Restoration Church International

Foreword for The Kingdom Leader in You

When Apostle Dr. Daniel Andrews asked me to write the foreword for this book, *The Kingdom Leader in You: What to Know as You Grow*, I received it not just as an honor, but as a divine assignment. I have had the privilege of knowing and laboring in ministry alongside Dr. Andrews for many years. We have traveled the world together, preaching the Gospel, equipping leaders, and witnessing the transforming power of God touch lives and churches across nations. Through it all, I have seen his integrity, humility, and unwavering passion for building the Kingdom of God.

Dr. Andrews is not only a gifted teacher, prophet, and apostolic leader he is a man of deep prayer and genuine compassion. His life and ministry exemplify what it means to *lead by the Spirit and serve with the heart of Christ*. This book is a reflection of that heart. Within these pages, you will not only learn principles of leadership but encounter a fresh impartation of Kingdom truth that will shape your character and strengthen your calling.

In *The Kingdom Leader in You*, Dr. Andrews reveals that true leadership begins in the secret place — in listening to the voice of God before giving direction to others. His teachings on King David and King Solomon remind us that effective leadership is generational; it's about preparing others to carry the vision forward with faithfulness and precision. As Dr. Andrews so powerfully shows, David didn't force his way into leadership he paved the way. That is the essence of Kingdom leadership: building beyond yourself.

Having walked with Dr. Andrews through many seasons of ministry, I can attest that the wisdom found in this book has been lived before it was written. He leads with integrity, mentors with patience, and ministers with grace. His words carry weight because they come from experience and revelation.

I believe *The Kingdom Leader in You* will become a timeless resource for pastors, leaders, and believers who desire to fulfill their divine purpose. It will challenge you to *know your calling, face your battles, and lead with purpose.* My prayer is that as you read, the Spirit of God will awaken the leader within you not just to lead people, but to transform lives for the glory of God's Kingdom.

Apostle Dr. Brian Alton

Presiding Bishop, I.C.A.L.M. International Covering Alliance & Licensing for Ministries Founder, Chancellor, Gateway International Bible Institute Founder, Apostle, Restoration Church International – Peoria, Arizona

Table of Contents

Preface

Leadership is not a title it is a calling. It is forged in the quiet places of prayer, tested in the fires of adversity, and proven in the posture of service. Over the years, I have come to believe that every person is called to lead in some capacity. Whether in the home, the workplace, the church, or the community, leadership is not reserved for the few—it is entrusted to the faithful.

This book was born out of a deep conviction: that leadership is not about power, but about purpose. It is not about being elevated, but about lifting others. Through seasons of joy and sorrow, clarity, and confusion, I have witnessed firsthand the refining journey of leadership. I have faced opposition, wrestled with suffering, and learned that true victory comes not through dominance, but through surrender.

My prayer is that these pages will serve as a guide, a mirror, and a mantle. May they challenge you to lead with integrity, endure with grace, and serve with humility. Whether you are just beginning your journey or have walked many miles, may you find strength, wisdom, and encouragement here.

Chapter 1
Better Than Rubies

"For wisdom is better than rubies......." (Proverbs 8:11)

I have reached my mid-fifties now and see the next few years leading me into my sixties, which has caused me to reflect a little deeper and view things from a different perspective. I believe as we get older, we start to shift how we see things and how we react to things. It is true that you gain wisdom over the years, especially through trial and error. The things I used to do as a younger leader, I no longer do as a little bit older leader.

Through life experience, we can gain wisdom, which then manifests as maturity. As children or when we were younger, we did things with impulse and self-centeredness. Life has a way of growing us up. We learn from our mistakes.

The Apostle Paul would write,

When I was a child, I spoke as a child, I understood as a child, I thought as a child; but when I became a man, I put away childish things (I Corinthians 13:11).

I will be honest, when I was a younger leader, my decisions were based on reacting to what I heard instead of listening to understand, based upon my immaturity, inexperience, and at times pride.

As a young leader, you just want people to follow your instructions without feedback. Hearing what people are saying and getting their input can help you make the right decisions. I felt I had all the answers, which I found out I do not. That takes the pressure off when you lead with transparency.

When I reflect on those days, I wish I had done things a bit differently. However, they have become learning moments for what I do now. Today, I have been told that I carry the wisdom of God. The scriptures teach us, "If any of you lacks wisdom, let him ask of God, who gives to all liberally and without reproach, and it will be given to him" (James 1:5). My desire now is to carry wisdom; **leaders should be seekers of wisdom.** Solomon himself understood what was important when it came to leading others after God appeared and said to Solomon, "Ask for whatever you want me to give you" (II Chronicles 1:7). Solomon would reply after praising God, "Give me wisdom and knowledge that I may go out and come in before this people; for who can judge this great people of yours." (II Chronicles 1:10).

Solomon had a great task. This was not just about power, ruling, or great possession; it was a call to shepherd a people. David, his father, before being anointed as king, was a shepherd. I believe in Christian leadership, whether in the church or in the corporate world. God wants leaders to be shepherds. Guiding, protecting, and yes, disciplining if necessary. Riches and wealth come with it as well. As we see in Solomon's case, he asked for wisdom first, and God honored him with riches. Please note verses 10 and 11. His posture was about humility, see 1 Kings 3:7-8. Scripture teaches that when we exalt ourselves, we will be made humbled; if we humble ourselves, we will be exalted (Matthew 23:12).

Wisdom is more precious than any expensive jewel, **"For wisdom is better than rubies, and all the things one may desire cannot be compared with her" (Proverbs 8:11).**

Earthly riches are fleeting, often tied to status or material gain. Wisdom, by contrast, builds legacy, aligns with God's will, and multiplies impact across generations. An account in the Bible shares about storing up treasures in heaven, not on the earth, where moths and rust destroy (Matthew 6:19-21). Please note that material possession is not wrong, and having money is okay because it has a way of helping and opening doors; it is not wrong to have riches. It is the LOVE of money that is the root of all kinds of evil (I Tim 6:10). Money can be lost and money can be stolen, but wisdom protects us; however, money cannot. The scriptures tell us that God gives us the power to create wealth, Deut. 8:18. Wisdom helps us maintain wealth and helps us make the right decisions with it.

Wisdom will keep you out of a lot of trouble and help you make the right decisions.

Many times, I would say to my children, protect your name, be honest in your business, never cheat to get your way with people, because when your name and reputation get damaged, it is hard to recover. The scriptures teach us, "A good name is to be chosen rather than great riches, loving favor rather than silver and gold" (Proverbs 22:1).

I can only think of what I told them regularly, that there are consequences to our decisions, whether right or wrong. When we make good decisions, good things happen. When we make bad decisions, bad things happen. Also, show me your friends and I will show you your future. Evil company corrupts good habits. (I Cor 15:33)

A good leader is always imparting wisdom, leading, and teaching others not to make mistakes he or she might have made along the journey to their own success.

Wisdom will help us see things differently in the light of eternity because no matter how long we live, it can never be compared to eternity. I could live to a hundred years, and it still cannot be compared to eternity. When I am gone, what legacy will I leave for others to follow? Wisdom is teaching me more about how to handle what has been entrusted to me and what will be given to me, and what will await me after I leave this earth. Being a leader does not mean just to lead for today; it means building for eternity. Their decisions shape generations, their obedience becomes a legacy, and their wisdom is shaped by the One who sees the end from the beginning. We only have a short time on earth, so what is given is temporary. The New American Standard Bible renders it this way,

"For we must all appear before the judgment seat of Christ, so that each one may receive compensation for his deeds done through the body, in accordance with what he has done, whether good or bad" (II Corinthians 5:10, NASB).

The word compensation here can mean payment, so we will receive payment for the good and the bad for what we have done on the earth through our bodies. That is why we must keep eternity in perspective, and everything we do must be in the light of eternity because that is what matters the most in the end. Wisdom reminds us that investing in the Kingdom of God will always produce eternal rewards. Our eternal rewards will go on forever, but that will require us to use wisdom now. We have been given stewardship over the things we have now, and wisdom will guide us in the process of how we are to be good stewards over our life, family, finances, and even our health. According to Merriam-Webster dictionary, the word stewardship means "the conducting, supervising, or managing of something" (Merriam-Webster, 2022). Even in scripture, as you read in Ephesians chapter three verse two, the word dispensation means administration of a household or estate, economy, or stewardship

(Blueletterbible, 2022). **So, according to the context of those who lead, we must be good stewards in this dispensation of time that was given to us in leading the affairs of God.**

Let me remind you that salvation is a free gift. However, the word seat in II Corinthians 5:10 in Greek is Bema (Bay-ma), which means to step one's foot on (like stepping onto something like a platform). This word can also give us an understanding of a tribunal. Therefore, we will account for our time spent, how we steward our time, our gifts, and people, etc., in this body on earth. It is not punishment. It is like when I get hired for a job, they give a performance review of my work, and then reward me for it. If I do not do a good job, I do not get rewarded or recognized. That is why we must keep eternity in view. Another example: When my wife and I were pastoring, we would have special events. Though everyone was invited to the event and it was free. There were those in the congregation who would help us prepare, set up, etc. During the event, we would give them a special honor by recognizing them. So, salvation determines where you go for eternity. Eternal rewards are recognized for how you lived as part of the family of God. Also, Scripture references the 5 Crowns we will receive.

1) Crown of life (James 1:12; Rev 2:10).
2) Incorruptible Crown (I Cor 9:24-25).
3) Crown of Rejoicing (I Thessalonians 2:19).
4) Crown of Glory (I Peter 5:1-4).
5) Crown of Righteousness (II Tim 4:6-8).

As we lead, are we seeking the wisdom of God? Are we conducting our affairs according to His wisdom? Are we being good stewards in those things entrusted to us? As leaders, we are entrusted with people. So, wisdom reminds us that we should be raising and training people to step up or in as we move on, or even when we leave this earth. The next generation is also entrusted to us as leaders.

Stewardship

We cannot ask people to do things that we would not do ourselves. Mentoring falls in line with the book, preparing others. Eventually, we move on or pass away. Everything is temporary; what is given is for stewardship purposes. When others see us being good stewards, they will follow the example. It all starts with the leader. Stewardship demands we do the right thing.

God will always leave the next generation a work to do, and not just leave everything for us to do. Good leaders are always looking ahead. They have vision and, at the same time, inspire others to catch the vision. Leaders encourage others, push people to maximize their given potential, and do not squander opportunities.

Be available, be approachable. Select someone to impart wisdom. The more you show availability and being approachable, you will find a person that you can begin to mentor. Find the person who wants what you can impart.

Complacency is a thief of the kingdom impact. It is important not to rest in comfort or trade comfort for conviction or routine over revelation, Leaders never stay comfortable.

See the Potential

I remember my spiritual father came to me while I was with the Assemblies of God. He saw the call on my life and knew I had the gift of teaching. So, he came and said, "Dan, I want you to start teaching the adult Sunday school class." I swallowed a bit and said, "Really?" My emotion was one of fear, and I thought, what am I doing here? I thought I would get shredded to pieces by these individuals afterwards. This wisdom I received was before the Sunday school class when my spiritual Father asked me to do this class. He imparted wisdom to me. He told me not to worry, but study the curriculum because even though they are professors, they just did not show up with the knowledge, they had to study. He also told me to stay teachable, and you will go far. So, their comments may seem criticism, but they were not. It turned out that they were very impressed by me in each class.

You see, this Sunday school class was in the sanctuary where all the theologians and professors from the local Christian college came. They all attended this Sunday school class and, at times, taught the class. Now, I was going to go in there and teach all these professors who had more years of experience than I. So, there I was teaching scholars of the Bible, and in the end, I had a blast. Each week, the sanctuary would be packed with new people and teachers. One of them even came up to me and said, "You taught things I had never seen before," and said my teaching was at a college level.

Leaders see the potential in people, and they lead them, teach them, and even show them how to walk in their calling. Good leaders see the gift in others and encourage them to stir up that gift.

The Apostle Paul would write to his beloved spiritual son,

"Therefore, I remind you to stir up the gift of God which is in you through the laying on of my hands. For God has not given us a spirit of fear, but of power and of love and of a sound mind" (II Timothy 1:6-7).

The Apostle Paul called Timothy his true Son in the faith (I Timothy 1:2). Leadership is about multiplication. It is not about position but multiplication. Jesus would say Make disciples of all nations (Matthew 28:19).

The leader, spiritual father, coming out of Paul, reminds his spiritual son not to neglect that gift in you. That gift was imparted to be used, not to burn out.

We are called to recognize, affirm, and activate the gifts in those we lead. The Spirit God gives is not timid; it is bold, empowering, and contagious. When leaders stir others, they multiply impact, awaken dormant callings, and release a generation into divine purpose. As I indicated, my Spiritual Father saw something in me, I did not see myself, and he believed in me and was always encouraging and challenging me. As leaders, we need to encourage and challenge those who follow us, help them see their potential.

He reminds Timothy that if the fire is going out, fan the flame or resuscitate it!

Some of us just need a fresh windblown on the embers to rekindle the fire again, and many times that comes through the encouraging words of our leaders

Good leaders are never jealous and are never envious; they are secure in their own success and secure in themselves.

John Maxwell has a book called "The Leadership Handbook: 26 Critical Lessons Every Leader Needs.' He writes in his book that "A leader's credibility begins with personal success. It ends with helping others achieve personal success" (Maxwell, 2008, p 4). My spiritual father became successful in his ministry, so he wanted me to be successful in the one I would embark on. I cut my teeth in ministry with the Assemblies of God under a great leader, and I will always be grateful for the opportunities and teaching that I received and the mentoring I received while we were there. We need more good spiritual leaders; they are needed more in today's day and age. I remember when my son was in wrestling and football, I was always pacing the sidelines. I was always there to give my advice, encouragement, and at times, protect him when I thought he was being treated unfairly. When I thought he was out of line with his sportsmanship, I would correct him. The Bible teaches us, "But if you are without chastening, of which all have become partakers, then you are illegitimate and not sons" (Hebrews 12:8). When we receive correction, that means we are true sons and a good father corrects his son, and a good son receives that correction. "A wise son heeds his father's instructions: but a scorner does not listen to rebuke" (Proverbs 13:1).

God can speak in many ways to his church, so that he should be made known to rulers and authorities. In Ephesians 3:10, it speaks of the manifold wisdom of God. Manifold in the Greek means multifaceted, richly diverse, many-sided. So, God's wisdom is not one-dimensional. So, through prayer, scripture, godly counsel, the Spirit, and through life experience, we can find God's wisdom. Practically, we pray, search the word, wait on the Spirit, and seek Godly counsel. Jesus is both the power and the wisdom of God, (I Cor 1:24).

Reflection Questions:

- In what areas of your life are you reacting rather than listening to understand?
- What does choosing wisdom over recognition look like in your current leadership role?

Prayer for Wisdom

Prayer: You have said, if anyone lacks wisdom, let him ask, and so I come, not in strength, but in need. I acknowledge where my insight falls short, where my understanding is clouded, and where my steps feel uncertain. Yet I do not come in fear, for You are the God who gives generously, without rebuke, without hesitation. Pour out Your wisdom upon me, not just for knowledge, but for discernment. Let me see as You see, choose as You would choose, and walk in paths that reflect Your heart. Remove the fog of confusion and replace it with clarity rooted in Your Word.

Putting it into Practice

- **Leadership Truth:** Your reputation often goes before you; people will hear about you before they meet you.
- **Practical Step (Reflection):** Take time to reflect on how others might describe your character. What do they say about your integrity, attitude, or trustworthiness?
- **Leadership Truth:** Lead as if every action you take has eternal weight and impact.

- **Practical Step (Action):** Identify one area of your life where you need a bigger, eternal perspective (not just short-term gain). Then, surrender that area to God in prayer.
- **Leadership Truth:** A true leader does not just shine themselves; they help others discover and grow their gifts.
- **Practical Step (Action):** Encourage someone today in their calling. Point out a strength or gift you see in them and speak life into it.

Chapter 2
King David

King David gives us many examples of leadership, even when preparing the next generation. David would not be the one to build the temple, but that responsibility was left for Solomon to do. David would give Solomon the blueprints in which the Spirit of God had directed him to do (1 Chronicles 28:12). Leadership begins with listening. This models a posture of humility: true leadership starts with receiving, not asserting. The temple was to be a dwelling place for God, so its design had to reflect divine priorities. Likewise, Spirit-led leaders build ministries, teams, and strategies that reflect heaven's values, not just human ambition. Spirit-led leadership is generational. It equips others to carry the vision forward with precision and faithfulness. Before verse twelve, David would give his son an exhortation "Consider now, for the Lord has chosen you to build a house for the sanctuary; Be strong and do the work" (1 Chronicles 28:10).

Leaders must not just dream they must build. Vision without execution is just imagination. Leadership in Kingdom work demands courage, not just in facing opposition, but in staying faithful when the task feels overwhelming. Strength here is spiritual rooted in prayer, Scripture, and the assurance of divine calling.

God always leaves a work for the next generation. In 1 Chronicles 22:8, David recounts God's word to him: "You have shed much blood and have fought many wars. You are not to build a house for my Name…" So, God told David he would not. Solomon's name is rooted in *shalom*, meaning peace. His reign marked a shift from warfare to rest, aligning with the temple's purpose as a sanctuary of divine presence (1 Kings 5:3–5). David's role was not diminished; it was foundational. He prepared the materials, organized the Levites, and cast the vision (1 Chronicles 28). God's will often involve generational partnership. We must be obedient to what God has decided.

David, in accepting God's decision and supporting Solomon's mission, is a model of surrendered leadership. He did not force his way he paved the way. If we do not prepare for the next generation, everything will stop with us. David had the vision, but Solomon had to do the work. This models generational leadership: one lays the foundation, another builds. Leaders must act with legacy in mind what you build today shapes worship, wisdom, and witness.

Many times, we get upset that God did not choose us to do a work we thought we were intended to do; instead, He uses us to train up the ones whom God has chosen. David would make abundant preparation before his death (1 Chronicles 22:5).

David gathered materials for the temple; he did not leave Solomon empty-handed. Viewing succession not as retirement, but as release into greater purpose. David knew he would not build the Temple himself, but made sure his son Solomon could. David gave the blueprints, resources, vision, and encouragement. Good leaders are not afraid to pass the baton; they prepare others to run farther. We are to lead beyond ourselves. If your leadership ends with you, it was never about the kingdom. Before David would die, he would give his son Solomon final instructions, see 1 Kings 2: 2-4.

Good leadership leaves the blueprint for the next generation.

David was not the kind of leader who would say, Do as I say, not as I do. David knew it would need finances to build. David would not only ask for the leaders of Israel to give, but He would give of his own resources, and the result was that David and the people rejoiced and offered willingly (1 Chronicles 29:9). True leaders do not demand they demonstrate. This is the essence of authentic leadership: investing personally in the mission before inviting others to join. It builds trust, credibility, and momentum for leadership teams today. People will not follow a leader who will not walk the path they prescribe. Many leaders today falter because they ask for commitment without demonstrating it themselves. They preach sacrifice but protect comfort.

So many times, people in leadership ask people to give or sacrifice, but never do it themselves. David left the charge to Solomon to be strong and do the work, giving him confidence that God would be behind it all. It is not just what you accomplish it is what you equip others to continue. Mentorship matters: leaving blueprints means investing in people, not just projects. Good leaders are never threatened. David was a secure leader, always putting the right people around him and never being threatened by them because he knew the right people would help him in battle (1 Chronicles 12). 1 Chronicles 12 says that those who joined David could shoot arrows from their bows with either their right or left hand (Ambidextrous). They could also sling stones the same way (V 2). There were also brave soldiers of valor trained in war and skilled with the shield and spear (V-8). David used it all to his advantage, even if they were better warriors than he was. Celebrate their success, even when it outshines yours. You delegate authority, not just tasks.

Good leaders always have good people around them so they can receive counsel from them.

The scriptures teach us, "Where there is no counsel, the people fall; But in the multitude of counselors there is safety" (Proverbs 11:14). Without wise counsel, decisions become narrow, reactive, and risky. Diverse perspectives refine vision and prevent blind spots. David would cast the vision before the people of Israel to get behind the building. He also reminds them that they need to help Solomon because he was inexperienced (I Chronicles 29:1). Let them face challenges without interruption. Give them a foundation to build upon.

Good leaders cast the vision because the scriptures say, "Where there is no vision, the people perish" (Proverbs 29:18). We must give confidence to those who would come up underneath us and continue the work of the Lord, and not just think it ends when we end. Leaders build, and as we see, David was a builder; he had the blueprints given by the Spirit. **Leaders build, and we see it throughout our scriptures; leaders are builders.**

The mission statement for my ministry at one point was doing R.E.P.S.

Reach, Equip, Prepare, Send.

Good leaders prepare people for the things ahead, through equipping, training, and leaving behind a legacy.

The scripture tells us, "A good man leaves an inheritance to his children's children" (Proverbs 13:22). This goes beyond just monetary things but wealth of knowledge, wisdom, skills, and yes, finances to help those who come from us, whether natural children or spiritual children. This is part of leaving a legacy and training up the next generation. As I mentioned previously, David had the right people to join him in battle.

It is very important we find the right people to help us in the battle of life, but not just in battle, but in the joys of life as well. We need those who have our heart and catch on to our vision, people who can carry the vision with you. Those you can trust and those who have your back in the heat of battle.

Practical Application

- In what ways does the Exhortation "Be strong and do the work" reflect God's continual command for His people to have courage in carrying out His purposes? (1 Chronicles 28:10; Joshua 1:9).
- Why is it important for leaders to recognize God has chosen someone else for a task, as David did with Solomon, and how does this reflect humility? (1 Chronicles 28:6; Numbers 27:18–23 with Joshua and Moses).
- How does the principle "Where there is no vision, the people perish" (Proverbs 29:18) challenge leaders to continually cast God's vision before their people?
- What does Solomon's inexperience (1 Chronicles 29:1) teach us about the need for older generations to guide and equip younger ones in faith and leadership? (Titus 2:1–8).

Prayer

Lord, may our leadership be marked not by control, but by commissioning.

Help us discern whether we are truly equipping or merely maintaining influence.

Expose every place where fear masquerades as stewardship, and replace it with trust in Your design.

Putting It into Practice

- Have you ever felt disappointed when God did not choose you for a task you thought was yours? How did you respond?
- Who are the "Solomons" in your life that God has called you to prepare?
- Do you feel secure in your leadership, or do you sometimes feel threatened by the strengths of others?
- If your leadership ended today, what "blueprints" would you like to leave behind for those who follow?

Chapter 3
Moses

I want us to look at several accounts of Moses when it comes to knowing who is with you as leaders and who is with you in battle. The first Account is found in Exodus 17, while the people of Israel were still at Rephidim (resting place). Rephidim is where the Israelites rested during their exodus from Egypt. Moses, by God's command, struck the rock, and water came out of the rock. The Apostle Paul would write of the account in I Corinthians, "And all of them drank from the spiritual Rock that traveled with them, and that Rock was Jesus" (I Corinthians 10:4). What I thought is interesting was that Paul said the Rock traveled with them. Did this rock go wherever they went, providing water to the people? Jesus said about those who thirst, "If anyone thirsts, let him come to Me and drink" (John 7:37). Now, while the people of Israel were in Rephidim, Amalek came and fought with Israel (Exodus 17:8-9). Amalek and the Amalekites were the relentless enemies of God's People. Moses would tell Joshua, "Choose us some men and go out, fight with Amalek. "Tomorrow I will stand on the top of the hill with the rod of God in my hand" (Exodus 17:9). Joshua would do as Moses commanded and went out and fought Amalek, while Moses, Aaron, and Hur went to the top of the hill. Now, if Moses was able to keep his Hands up with the rod of God, Israel prevailed. But when Moses' hands would drop, Amalek prevailed (Exodus 17:11-12). Moses became weary so Aaron and Hur placed a rock underneath Moses and Held up his arms one on each side of Moses (Exodus 17:12). They would stay there until the sun went down and Joshua would defeat Amalek and His people with a sword (Exodus 17:13). I learned that having others pray for you gives strength and courage in the fight, reminding you that you are not alone. The presence of Aaron and Hur reminds us no leader can do anything alone. Behind every leader is a team. A good team can help a leader succeed. People we can trust are so important today because everyone has an agenda. What do we learn from this account regarding finding the right people to stand with you as you lead?

First, knowing those who are alongside you is crucial in helping you stay strong in the face of adversity.

This was a team effort; Joshua did as Moses commanded. There are times we must go out and fight the battle. Moses was there to encourage Joshua in the fight. Moses, the leader, stood for Joshua and the people. Yet Moses had Aaron and Hur to stand with him. Leaders need people to stand and encourage them as well.

Secondly, knowing those who are alongside you is crucial in helping you stay strong in the battle and in your victories.

There is an advantage when we support our leaders. There is an advantage when our leaders intercede for us; leaders are there to cover and encourage. The scriptures teach us, "Obey those who rule over you, and be submissive, for they watch out for your souls, as those who must give account. Let them do so with joy and not with grief, for that would be unprofitable for you" (Hebrews 13:17). There are benefits when we support our leaders, and we should do it with joy because it is unprofitable if you bring grief to them. Speaking well of them in their absence builds trust and strengthens their reputation. We can encourage them by simply serving them and honoring them.

Finally, knowing those who are alongside you is crucial in helping you remain victorious in your battles.

Moses had Aaron and Hur; they stood alongside him until the sun went down. Joshua was able to be victorious because Moses was able to intercede.

The wrong people will hurt you in the long run; many will come alongside you, but they do not have your heart and your well-being in mind. I speak from experience, a few times we dealt with those who said they were with us to find out they were just trying to get close enough to us, just to hurt us. However, some were glad in their hearts to help carry our vision. Which brings me to the second account concerning Moses. Before leading the people of God out of Egypt, Moses would have his encounter with God. Now, Moses would begin to converse back and forth with God, and Moses' conversation was one of doubt. This conversation and interaction got heated, God got angry with Moses because of what Moses said, "O my Lord, please send by the hand of whomever else you may send" (Exodus 4:13). God's anger was kindled against Moses (Exodus 4:14). He would remind Moses of his brother and that He can speak well, and he is coming out to meet you and when he sees you, he will be glad in his heart (Exodus 4:14). Aaron was glad in his heart because he had Moses's heart in mind. It would be a joy for him to serve Moses and to be his spokesman. This is key to having those around us as leaders who will help you and have joy doing it. We need those around us who will be good spokesmen for us in ministry, the workplace, and in our personal lives. We need those who are not easily persuaded by the trickery of men or the evil intentions of those who wish us ill will. Those who truly have your heart in mind are honest, care about how they treat your family, and stand with you when needed. They are invested in your purpose, not just their own. Many who are overly nice or constantly say 'I love you' often do so with an agenda. I was fortunate to have many Aarons in my life who were glad to be alongside us. Now,

Good leaders do not control but trust those around them, so they delegate. Moses's father-in-law imparts some good advice to Moses,

So, Moses' Father-in-Law said to him,

The thing that you do is not good. Both you and these people who are with you will surely wear yourselves out. For this thing is too much for you; you are not able to perform it by yourself. Listen to my voice; I will give you counsel, and God will be with you… (Exodus 18:17-19).

We must learn for the sake of our health and well-being; delegating is a responsibility of a good leader.

When leaders delegate with confidence, they affirm the value and capability of their team. Authority Unlocks Initiative: A trusted team member with delegated authority can adapt, innovate, and lead others. It creates a ripple effect of empowerment. Leaders delegate roles in planning, design, and execution while maintaining spiritual oversight. Leaders give them authority to make decisions.

It not only keeps us from burning out, but it says to those we delegate responsibility too that we trust them with. Many walk away simply because they became overwhelmed with their circumstances or tired because they are left to do everything. Many leaders who do not delegate or trust in delegating have a sense of fear of others getting it wrong. Or many times, fear of people look to others instead of you. They may have a fear of others looking better than they do. There is also a sense of having a controlling spirit. Pride also has a reason behind it. Leaders create space and do not micromanage everything. Leaders train, educate, celebrate wins, whether big or small, and most importantly trust. Many times, church leaders walked away, never to serve again; some have gone as far as committing suicide. This is a tragedy of epic proportions when someone who has committed their life to serving others takes their life because the stress becomes overwhelming. We need more people praying, supporting, and helping our leaders who watch over us. They not only watch over our souls, but they also have their own responsibilities at home; they have a family. We tend to ignore that they are human beings, and they have a soul, and that soul, if not careful, can be wounded like anyone else. It is important to have good intercessors and a support system around you as leaders, where you can share your burden and not carry it around like dead weight. People will have the tendency to back their dump truck up and dump everything on you for you to clean up and fix the mess, and when you do not, it is your fault. If we are not careful, we will become pallbearers for the dead; we carry them around as they lie dead on you until you are six feet under. I received this personal word from the Lord about being a pallbearer some time ago. The word was this: the word of the Lord came to me and said, you were not called to be a pallbearer. I did not call you to carry around dead things. Those who do not wish to know me, those who desire their flesh over me, those who do not contribute, give, follow, or even listen to the one I have sent, move on, stop carrying those who desire to be dead.

Jesus would even speak to this in Luke's gospel, Jesus said to him, "Let the dead bury their own dead, but you go and preach the kingdom of God" (Luke 9:60). This is a powerful statement that today's culture would call insensitive. We are not called to carry the dead but to raise the dead from their spiritual death that they are living in. The Bible says that we are walking dead men without Christ, "And you He made alive, who were dead in trespasses and sins" (Eph 2:1). John 5 tells us, "Most assuredly, I say to you, he who hears My word and believes in Him who sent Me has everlasting life, and shall not come into judgment, but has passed from death into life" (John 5:24). Jesus said in Luke 9:60, "But you go and preach the Kingdom of God." As we go preaching the Kingdom, the power of darkness is cast out. We are not called to carry the dead around but bring the life-giving message of the Kingdom. We are called to bring people into the life-giving Gospel of Jesus Christ and not leave them in their grave clothes. We carry people around who do not care, give, or even participate. Many times, people will use up your time when it comes to prayer and counsel just to repeat the process with you. The purpose is to wear you down, burn you out, so you too become as dead as they are. Many times, there is a spirit behind this tactic. Remember, it is not the person operating; it is the spirit behind it, wanting to burn you out. The gift of discerning of spirits (1 Cor. 12:10) allows leaders to perceive whether a situation is influenced by the Holy Spirit, human emotion, or demonic interference. We sometimes tolerate the demon instead of casting out the demon. Jesus never counseled or even gave demons a moment of His time.

The man or woman of God who leads, care for the flock of God, cares for their own home, and then deals with darkness, shoulders a great load. Prayer is just the beginning of how we can support them. As leaders, we must discern the pressures of tough situations. We must keep our guard up against the enemy's schemes. We must also, protect ourselves from the pressure from others that would cause us to yield to the pressure. When feeling the pressure, we must keep in mind there are some things not to do and some things to do when we find ourselves in high-pressure situations.

Lessons on Leadership Character

- From Moses's doubts to God providing Aaron as a spokesman, what lessons do you take away about the importance of humility and trust?
- How do you see the connection between trust and delegation in leadership?
- What risks do leaders face when they try to control instead of trust those around them?

Practical Application

- If you could summarize the leadership lesson of Moses at Rephidim in one sentence, what would it be?
- How do you see the principles in this chapter applying to your personal leadership role—whether at home, work, or ministry?
- What safeguards can you put in place today to avoid becoming spiritually or emotionally burned out as a leader?
- Who have been your "Aaron and Hur" in your leadership journey, and how did they help you remain strong?

Chapter 4
Pressure

In the book of Exodus, Moses and the children of Israel find themselves up against the wall. Exodus 14 explains a very high-pressure situation that Moses and the people of Israel would face while at the Red Sea. Moses and the people of Israel are pinned down, with nowhere to turn as Pharaoh and his army advance on them. The people start to cry out to the Lord, and then they start blaming Moses. As we know, when things go wrong, the Leader is always the one they turn to blame.

The buck always stops with the one in charge, no matter what level of leadership you are in.

Now, they say to Moses, "For it would have been better for us to serve the Egyptians than that we should die in the wilderness" (Exodus 14:12). Moses would give the people of Israel one of the most powerful statements ever, in my opinion, when he said,

Do not be afraid. Stand still, and see the salvation of the Lord, which He will accomplish for you today. For the Egyptians whom you see today, you shall see them no more forever. The Lord will fight for you, and you shall hold your peace. (Exodus 14:13-14).

Moses did not panic; he trusted God's guidance. His calmness stemmed from spiritual alignment, not self-reliance. Leaders grounded in purpose or values can remain steady when circumstances shake. Moses gave clear instructions: "Stand still and see the salvation of the Lord." He did not add confusion; he simplified. In a crisis, clarity is more powerful than being charismatic. Leaders must boil down complexity into an actionable direction. Pressure prompts action; it has a way of exposing what is really in us. We either react or act. When we feel the pressure financially, emotionally, or spiritually, we are tempted to retreat to what is familiar, even if it was harmful. Remember, Egypt represented bondage, but in their panic, it looked like safety. But God did not bring them out of Egypt to go back. He brought them out to move forward. And that's where Moses speaks a word that still echoes today: "Stand still and see the salvation of the Lord." In other words, do not let pressure push you into panic. After Moses told them to be still, God said, "Why are you crying out to me? Tell the people to move forward." Some would say—which is it, stand still or move forward? The understanding of the phrase "to stand still" is to hold your peace, be steadfast. The word "stand" in Hebrew is "yatsab," which means to trust and see, not to panic, but to watch and see. So, we are to trust and watch God work in our lives. Another reality is that we sometimes pray for a breakthrough, but God is waiting on us to take a step. The miracle did not come until Moses acted by raising his staff. The Red Sea did not split while they stood back; it parted when Moses raised his staff. This was an act of faith, and when we act in faith, the supernatural responds. So, pressure is often the very thing that prompts our action. Without it, we might stay stuck. Without it, we might never move. At times, God may use pressure to direct us, refine our faith, and prepare us for His power. The same sea that threatened to drown them became the path to their deliverance. Pressure does not mean God has left; it means He is setting the stage for something greater. Moses did not abandon his mission despite the people's complaints. A leader must remember the "why" behind their role and decisions. Purpose provides resilience when approval fades. Criticism often contains truth, even if it is wrapped in emotion or fear. Moses listened to the people's grievances even when they were harsh, and brought them before God. Leaders should seek understanding before reacting. In a crisis, people look to leaders for emotional cues. If a leader panics, the group spirals. Moses often responded with prayer and deliberation, not impulsive action.

The Lord responds with a very profound and interesting statement, "Why do you cry to Me? Tell the children of Israel to go forward. But lift your rod and stretch out your hand over the sea and divide it" (Exodus 14:15-16). We see that God tells the people to go forward when they are facing a body of water. How can they move forward? God was waiting for Moses to make his move. I have heard countless times in church meetings all over the world, the people crying out to the Lord God move on our behalf, or we are waiting on a move of God. When all the while God is waiting for us to move, God already revealed to Moses what He would do through the staff when He said What is that in your hand? and Moses would reply to the Lord, a staff (Exodus 4:2). Often, the "rod" is something familiar like Moses's staff that has been with you all along. It may be a skill, relationship, or spiritual authority that has proven effective in past seasons. The rod can represent what God had given. God has given everyone a gift that is to be used. God can take an ordinary thing you may have and use His power through it. Leadership requires boldness, and God gave Moses the authority to be bold. Action can get results, while being passive can cause a breakdown in trust. Passive leadership will cause havoc in a company and a church. Giving people grace is one thing, but being passive will allow others to usurp your authority, as you will see in my description of Jezebel in a later chapter. God does not want passive leaders. He wants faithful ones. Leaders who pray and act. Who waits and moves. Who listens and leads. Another thought is that those who overthink, could you imagine what would have happened to Moses if he had overthought what God wanted him to do at the Red Sea? At times, we must be decisive in our actions and decisions.

Vision keeps the people from perishing (Proverbs 29:18). Faith-filled words fuel the vision. Hebrews 11:1 reminds us that faith is the substance of things hoped for, the evidence of things not seen. Vision begins with believing in what God has revealed, even before it manifests. Proverbs 18:21 says, "death and life are in the power of the tongue." Speaking faith-filled words reinforces the vision and keeps it alive. We are to speak life into our vision and plans.

Some situations require immediate action, trusting God to guide as you go. The vision is what guides the decision. Every church and company have a vision or mission statement that can guide its decisions.

I really believe in many cases God is waiting for us to move, and when we move, He will respond with supernatural power. God would do His part as Moses would do his when he stretched out his hands over the sea, and the Lord caused the sea to part (Exodus 14:21). As leaders, we must be living out what we are teaching. Leaders must often take the first step, even when the path ahead seems impossible. Faith and action go hand in hand. Moses's action was a demonstration of faith. He did not part the sea himself, but he had to do his part. Leadership is not about controlling outcomes; it is about doing what is required, trusting that others (or God, in this context) will respond. Moses was leading a people. His obedience was not just personal; it was on behalf of others. Leaders carry the weight of their decisions. Personal responsibility means recognizing that your actions affect those who follow you.

Faith is active. The miracle waited until their movement. Sometimes God will not move the obstacle until we move our feet. Action is putting feet to our faith. The Israelites had to start moving through the parted waters. Unfortunately for many, seeing is believing. The Israelites had already seen the miracles that got them to this place. So, we can say Moses had proven his leadership with God and the people before. Good leaders with good track records will have better results in people trusting them. However, people can be very fickle as in the case of the Israelites. They saw Moses perform miracles and still questioned him. Leadership is not for the faint of heart.

The danger of looking back is that Egypt represented bondage, and the familiar can keep us from growing. Stagnation can keep growth from happening. Fear of the unknown or fear of making a mistake can prevent us from moving forward. This is represented in Numbers Chapter 13, when the 12 spies went out to survey the land, fear and disunity were represented in this chapter, even though there was evidence of the land flowing with milk and honey. Only Joshua and Caleb believed in what God promised; the other 10 gave a negative report that caused them to wander the wilderness. Now, what kept them from moving forward were the giants in that land. Many times, we are stuck because our situations feel like giants.

The bible teaches us, "But without faith it is impossible to please Him, for he who comes to God must believe that He is, and that He is a rewarder of those who diligently seek Him" (Hebrews 11:6). It is faith that will move God on our behalf as we move; He moves. Could it be that if Moses did not respond in faith by stretching out his hands, we could be telling a different story?

Our faith activates the supernatural power of God because it pleases Him, and when it pleases Him, we get rewarded!

The result was that the sea parted, and the people of God crossed in safety, and God closed the sea on the Egyptians. The pressure was causing them to return to bondage and be enslaved again, and the familiar spirit started to set in. God intends for us to move forward, not backwards, and yes, there will be some obstacles along the way. We must move in faith and trust the Lord to move on our behalf as we lead the people of God.

Reflection Questions

- Pressure situations often create opportunities for breakthroughs. What are some biblical or personal examples where pressure led to spiritual growth and leadership development?
- How can leaders train themselves and their people to see pressure not as a setback but as a setup for God's supernatural intervention?

Chapter 5
Absalom, Jezebel, Judas

Many times, leaders will encounter three oppositions: Absalom, Jezebel, and Judas. Now, Absalom was David's one son who had his brother killed for raping their sister (II Samuel 13).

Absalom would also commit treason against his father, David.

Oh, that I were made judge in the land, and everyone who has any suit or cause would come to me; then I would give him justice. And so it was, whenever anyone came near to bow down to him, that he would put out his hand and take him and kiss him. In this manner, Absalom acted toward all Israel who came to the king for judgment. So, Absalom stole the hearts of the men of Israel (II Samuel 15:4-6).

It is a common temptation that many believe they could lead better than the one currently entrusted with authority. In 2 Samuel 15:2, Absalom stationed himself at the city gate, intercepting those who came with complaints. He positioned himself as a sympathetic ear, subtly undermining King David's leadership by presenting himself as the people's advocate. This same spirit often surfaces in workplaces, churches, and ministries. When individuals feel unheard, misrepresented, or wounded by leadership decisions, an "Absalom" may arise, someone who carries personal grievances and uses them to build influence under the guise of advocacy. Their pain becomes a platform, and their charisma cloaks rebellion in concern. I have often said, "People build coalition to defend their grievances." These alliances are rarely born from pure motives; they are fueled by unresolved offense and a desire to correct perceived injustice.

Absalom himself was deeply wounded. His sister Tamar was raped by their half-brother Amnon, David's eldest son. David's failure to address and discipline this horrific act created a vacuum of justice and bred animosity within the family. Absalom's pain was real, but his response became a rebellion that fractured the kingdom. Let this be a sober reminder: unresolved wounds, when left unaddressed by leadership, can give rise to counterfeit advocates. And when discernment is lacking, the gate becomes a place of seduction rather than justice.

One of the key signs of an Absalom-like spirit is the appearance of public loyalty that masks private disloyalty. Such individuals often present themselves as spokespeople for the people, appearing knowledgeable, compassionate, and even helpful, yet their behavior behind the scenes tells a different story. They may openly correct or challenge leadership in public settings, subtly undermining authority while gaining influence. This behavior can be deeply deceptive, even fooling trusted members of your leadership team. Discernment is essential, as this spirit operates through charm, flattery, and the illusion of advocacy, all while sowing seeds of division and rebellion. Another observation would be how they treat your family. They may treat you one way and your family differently.

leaders often encounter manipulation and control in subtle yet persistent ways, including through financial giving. Some individuals may attempt to use their contributions as leverage, expecting influence, favoritism, or decision-making power in return. This form of control must be addressed swiftly and firmly. Leaders must recognize it as a spiritual tactic, not just a relational issue, and confront the controlling spirit with discernment, clarity, and biblical authority. Allowing such behavior to go unchecked can compromise the integrity of the ministry and distort the purpose of generosity. Giving should be an act of worship, not a tool for manipulation. It is not uncommon for individuals to approach leaders claiming, "God told me to be your intercessor." While this may sound spiritual, it can often be a subtle attempt to gain influence or control over your decisions. Rather than serving with humility, they may use spiritual language to push their own agenda, positioning themselves as a voice of authority in your life. They will say, "God told me…" but if God has not confirmed it to you, it is wise to pause and discern. True intercession is birthed in submission, not ambition. Leaders must be careful not to confuse spiritual flattery with divine assignment.

To guard against individuals with Absalom-like traits, those who subtly undermine leadership while appearing loyal. Spiritual leaders must cultivate discernment, relational transparency, and structural accountability. Absalom gained influence by exploiting emotional gaps and presenting himself as a more accessible alternative to King David (2 Samuel 15:1–6). Today's leaders must remain prayerful and vigilant, ensuring they are approachable and actively engaged with their teams and congregations. Establishing clear lines of authority, fostering a culture of honor, and addressing offenses biblically are essential to prevent manipulation and division. By discipling emerging leaders in servanthood rather than self-promotion, and by celebrating team victories over personal platforms, ministries can safeguard their mission and maintain unity. Ultimately, leaders must prioritize humility, clarity, and Kingdom-centered collaboration to resist the subtle seduction of Absalom's spirit.

We were always taught that an **Absalom spirit likes to get close to you, this spirit that operates in a person who uses false humility and, at times, wants to steal people's hearts away from God's appointed leader.** This spirit will always think they know more or even better than you when it comes to ministry, and quite frankly, in everything. I found an article by Dr. Dee Evans, who shares her perspective. She is an author, entrepreneur, consultant, and owner of Koinonia Training and Consulting, a consulting business that specializes in branding and life coaching (Evans, 2021).

This article helps explain more about this type of spirit.

Absalom is an impostor. People who possess the Absalom spirit are typically frustrated with the status of their life and with their perceived level in life. They frequently imagine they deserve more recognition than what their achievements merit. This can cause vendettas to be erected against individuals who visibly harness the favor of God, individuals of influence, as well as individuals who do not recognize them or honor them the way they perceive is just. As a tactic of warfare, the spirit of Absalom will deceive the individual operating within into embarrassing themselves by trying to accept (or steal) assignments that they are not anointed for (Evans, 2020).

I recall one time our worship leader at the time operated in an Absalom spirit. He would be very submissive to me and in front of other people, but behind the scenes, he was stealing hearts. People loved his singing, and they were drawn to him, as is the case with all worship leaders, and this is why worship leaders must maintain humility and guard their hearts. I started to notice his bizarre behavior. For instance, during announcements, while we were all sitting, I was in my normal seat up front. He squirmed his way up to the front and pulled a piece of lint from my shoe. I looked down at him, and he said there was some lint hanging off your shoe. There was another time when we were all in the classroom, where we would pray before the service. After we got done, I would let everyone go ahead of me, and I would walk out last. He then stopped me and brushed the shoulders of my sports coat and adjusted the lapels. After he did that, I started keeping my eye on him until the day he shoved my daughter in the sound booth. My wife went off on him, and I then called him later to have a meeting with the elders about the incident. I also had a list of questions concerning things that were getting back to me about what he was saying about the ministry. So, when we were together in my office, I started to ask him about what was being said, and of course, he denied each one. One of the things he was saying about me was that I was not really hearing from God. After asking all these questions, his reply was no to all of them, so I said Then you are calling everyone who came to me a liar? His reply, "I said none of those things." I got to the point of asking why you shoved my daughter. Then his true colors came out, he got up and screamed I knew you were going to ask me that! He pulled out the church key we gave him for worship practice, threw it on my desk, and said I was going to leave this church anyway! I replied, sit down and explain yourself, but he marched out the door, saying, go ahead and call the cops! That was the end of that; however, he had stolen the hearts of some of the people, but I was able to show them his intent, and they were shocked that they were being taken away by this spirit. Many times, we base our ministry on popularity, or we get drawn to the most popular person.

Jezebel

She wrote in the letters, saying,

Proclaim a fast, and seat Naboth with high honor among the people; and seat two men, scoundrels, before him to bear witness against him, saying, You have blasphemed God and the king. Then take him out, and stone him, that he may die (I Kings 21:9-10).

There is an interesting part to this passage concerning Jezebel.

She placed Naboth in a place of high honor, then used two individuals to accuse Him of cursing God. **This is deception at a high level, placing an individual in a seat of honor, then turning around and destroying the person.**

Control, jealousy, and power are always evidence of a Jezebel spirit. It seeks to destroy the reputations of others to get what it wants. The workplace is no different. This spirit also builds false accusations to hurt others. It will also build a coalition to support its action. (I Kings 21:10)

Many times, those who operate in these spirits will set you up to fail so that you do not look better than them. In my own experience, the ones who are always before the people, saying they love you and always saying, we honor you, are the ones to look out for. This Jezebel spirit is rooted in witchcraft, and witchcraft can really damage the mind of a person if they are not careful; it will cause distraction.

Do not lead passively. Ahab's passivity gave Jezebel the freedom to operate, ultimately enabling manipulation, idolatry, and spiritual corruption. When leaders abdicate their authority or avoid confrontation, they create an atmosphere where controlling spirits can thrive. Passive leadership does not just tolerate the Jezebel spirit;

it invites it. Spiritual authority must be exercised with clarity, conviction, and courage to protect the integrity of the ministry and the purity of its mission.

If a person around you begins to irritate you or begins to manipulate you through control, and it seems like there is an excuse every time something needs to be done, and you find yourself getting angry, and it consumes your mindset, this could be witchcraft.

Most individuals who get in front of the congregation and say We love you, seem to be the kiss of death because the very next week they would leave. Now, that is not to say that people who do say they love you are not sincere and genuine, but you can always sense the ones who are not. Love is an action word, and if we say we love someone, our actions will show it more than our words. The most quoted scripture ever tells us, "For God so loved the world that He gave His only begotten Son, that whoever believes in Him should not perish but have everlasting life" (John 3:16). Note, God loved the world, He gave His son. This was not mere words he displayed; He proved his love by giving us His son. Jesus reminds us that love is sacrificial, "Greater love has no one than this, than to lay down one's life for his friends" (John 15:13). So, the one who backs up his words is the ones who truly love you; their words match their actions.

Now, regardless of how we view each of these spirits, they are dangerous to leaders of churches and ministries. Yes, it can even happen in the secular world, even in the business realm.

Jezebel is always about power and control, and is always operating when there is a passive leader.

Ahab was passive and would allow Jezebel to run the show. let us look at the situation with Naboth again, prior to Jezebel setting up Naboth. Now Ahab bargained with Naboth, and the account reads like this,

And it came to pass after these things that Naboth the Jezreelite had a vineyard which was in Jezreel, next to the palace of Ahab, king of Samaria. So, Ahab spoke to Naboth, saying, give me your vineyard, that I may have it for a vegetable garden, because it is near, next to my house; and for it I will give you a vineyard better than it. Or, if it seems good to you, I will give you its worth in money. But Naboth said to Ahab, The Lord forbid that I should give the inheritance of my fathers to you! So, Ahab went into his house sullen and displeased because of the word which Naboth the Jezreelite had spoken to him; for he had said, I will not give you the inheritance of my fathers. And he lay down on his bed, and turned away his face, and would eat no food. But Jezebel, his wife, came to him, and said to him, why is your spirit so sullen that you eat no food? He said to her, Because I spoke to Naboth the Jezreelite, and said to him, give me your vineyard for money; or else, if it pleases you, I will give you another vineyard for it. And he answered, I will not give you my vineyard. Then Jezebel, his wife, said to him, you now exercise authority over Israel! Arise, eat food, and let your heart be cheerful; I will give you the vineyard of Naboth the Jezreelite (I Kings 21:1-7).

Ahab sulked like a child and whined to Jezebel about what had happened. Good leaders know how to take on tough situations and handle them with maturity and professionalism without building a coalition to come after someone else. Unfortunately, we like to get people on our side of things and get people to agree with us and see our position as being right and everyone else is wrong. Now, both individuals, Absalom, and Jezebel, faced their horrible demise in the end. Absalom's demise we read in II Samuel 18,

Then Absalom met the servants of David. Absalom rode on a mule. The mule went under the thick boughs of a great terebinth tree, and his head caught in the terebinth; so, he was left hanging between heaven and earth. And the mule which was under him went on. Now, a certain man saw it and told Joab, and said, I just saw Absalom hanging in a terebinth tree! Then Joab said, I cannot linger with you, and he took three spears in his hand and thrust them through Absalom's heart, while he was still alive in the midst of the terebinth tree. And ten young men who bore Joab's armor surrounded Absalom, and struck and killed him (II Samuel 18:9-10; 14-15).

We see Jezebel's account is found in II Kings 9,

So, they threw her down, and some of her blood spattered on the wall and on the horses; and he trampled her underfoot. And when he had gone in, he ate and drank. Then he said, go now, see to this accursed woman, and bury her, for she was a king's daughter. So, they went to bury her, but they found no more of her than the skull and the feet and the palms of her hands (II Kings 9:33-35).

Each of these individuals' lives ended horrifically and is a reminder to all of us not to partake, nor sit at the table of such spirits.

I had many encounters with these spirits; I was not what you call a passive leader when it comes to dealing with them. My wife and I were always dealing with women in the church who wanted to be Lynette and were bold enough to tell Lynette that. This is why a leader must always keep themselves on guard against the schemes of the devil. We had a woman one time say, you need to stop being up here with your husband and make room for others to be with Him. Lynette would respond by saying, excuse me, this is my husband! This individual was asked to leave until their heart gets right. I was always asked by other women who wanted me to counsel them, and I would say that is fine, but my wife is with me anytime I counsel someone of the other sex. She said, "I would just like for you to counsel me," to which my response was NO! After that, we would start getting mysterious calls at all hours of the day and night. Eventually, one day, she called and started screaming at my wife. I took the phone and told her not to call anymore. I had a meeting with this person with our administrator present because I did not want Lynette to be around this spirit anymore. I had to tell this individual to leave as well. We must deal with these kinds of spirits the right way. They seek to bring down leaders and, at times, eventually want to take over. Jesus Himself would face someone who would turn him in for thirty pieces of silver that would cost the Lord his life. Judas would be part of casting out demons and healing the sick, and yet turn on Jesus because, in the end, his heart was not pure.

Jesus would tell us,

Not everyone who says to Me, Lord, Lord, shall enter the kingdom of heaven, but he who does the will of My Father in heaven. Many will say to Me in that day, Lord, Lord, have we not prophesied in Your name, cast out demons in Your name, and done many wonders in Your name? And then I will declare to them, I knew you; depart from Me, you who practice lawlessness (Matthew 7:21-23).

Our motives and our hearts must be pure; this is why we must examine our hearts.

Judas

Judas would end up betraying Jesus with a kiss,

And while He was still speaking, behold, Judas, one of the twelve, with a great multitude with swords and clubs, came from the chief priests and elders of the people. Now his betrayer had given them a sign, saying, Whomever I kiss, He is the One; seize Him. (Matthew 26:47-48).

We once broke bread with people who shared in our deepest hurts and sacred moments, only to watch them turn against us, swayed by the spirit of Absalom and Jezebel. Yet through that betrayal, God taught me the value of discernment in what I share and with whom. Suffering is woven into the fabric of Kingdom leadership. If Christ Himself endured pain often at the hands of those closest, then we too must walk that path, trusting that even in suffering, His purpose prevails. Judas was placed there for a reason.

It is a painful thing to go through when individuals walk with you for a long period of time and then betray your trust. Once again, I found myself faced with a similar situation with an elder of our church, someone who believed in what we were doing and was there to help me lay the foundation of the ministry. He was even the first out of everybody to call me an apostle. Our families spent many days together. We ate together, prayed together, wept together, laughed together, and I even officiated his daughter's funeral, sharing great moments of powerful moves of God. However, the Absalom spirit stole his heart, and he turned on me and my wife. It was a betrayal that wounded us deeply because of our intimate relations with them. As leaders, we will find ourselves in the very place of Jesus, "He was despised and rejected by men, A Man of sorrows and acquainted with grief. And we hid, as it were, our faces from Him; He was despised, and we did not esteem Him" (Isaiah 53:3).

There are times when we will be despised and rejected and acquainted with grief because of the betrayal of people.

The Apostle writes, "For I consider that the sufferings of this present time are not worthy to be compared with the glory which shall be revealed in us" (Romans 8:18).

During our present suffering, we can expect a greater glory revealed in us.

The suffering we face is not to be compared because the greater the suffering, the greater the glory. Suffering can be in many ways and forms, and we can suffer under persecution. This glory will be revealed through us as we endure through the suffering. Many times, we ask God to take away the suffering, but God is looking at something greater, and that is His glory being manifested through us. When this glory is manifested, it shrinks the suffering so it cannot be compared to it. When Jesus was in Gethsemane, "And being in agony, He prayed more earnestly. Then His sweat became like great drops of blood falling to the ground" (Luke 22:44). His suffering caused Him to sweat blood; the redemption process had begun. What was lost in a garden was being redeem in a garden, His suffering was great to the point he would pray, "Father, if it is your will, take this cup away from me; nevertheless, not My will, but your will be done" (Luke 22:42). The cup would be the wrath that he would need to drink, He would bear the divine judgment that was meant for us. He would experience not only physical pain, but pain of separation from the Father. However, Jesus submitted to the Father's will and not His own. Through this process, the glory of God would be manifested through His death, burial, and resurrection.

Every step of the way Jesus submitted to the Fathers will, when He said, "Most assuredly, I say to you, the Son can do nothing of Himself, but what He sees the Father do; for whatever He does, the Son also does in like manner" (John 5:19). The scriptures also remind us, "And being found in appearance as a man, He humbled Himself and became obedient to the point of death, even the death of the cross" (Philippians 2:8). Many times, in our sufferings we want God to pull us out of the suffering. Now, we understand that Jesus was not only fully God, but also fully human. He felt the pain of suffering and even temptation. This is why we have a Savior that can relate to us, "For we do not have a High Priest who cannot sympathize with our weaknesses, but was in all points tempted as we are, yet without sin" (Hebrews 4:15).

When Jesus came out of the wilderness from being tempted by the devil, the scriptures tell us that He, "Returned in the power of the Spirit to Galilee, and news of Him went out through the surrounding regions. And he taught in their synagogues, being glorified by all" (Luke 4:14-15). The temptation he endured caused Him to return in the Power of the Spirit, and His name became famous throughout the regions. When we endure temptations and trust God to get us through them, we increase in the power of the Spirit, and in return, we make His name famous and bring glory to His name. Before his betrayal, Jesus would pray about bringing glory to the Father in John 17, "Father, the hour has come. Glorify Your Son, that Your Son also may glorify You" (John 17:1). The hour has come that we begin bringing glory to the Father. Manifesting His glory throughout the earth.

Reflection

- How can leaders stay alert and guard themselves from these three spirits (Absalom, Jezebel, Judas)?
- What role does accountability with elders, spouses, or mentors play in protecting leaders from spiritual attacks?
- How can churches or ministries create a culture where loyalty, humility, and love prevail over division and betrayal?
- How does the example of Jesus' submission to the Father's will encourage leaders facing suffering or betrayal?
- In what ways can suffering become a platform for God's glory to be revealed through your leadership?

Chapter 6
Accountability

The definition of accountability is this: "An obligation or willingness to accept responsibility or to account for one's actions" (Merriam-Webster, 2021). A leader's accountability is about responsibility. Responsibility in all our conduct and affairs of ministry and life. Responsibility is a core aspect of leadership, which means guiding others and making decisions that impact the team. Accountability goes a step further; it is about owning the outcomes, especially when things go wrong. A true leader does not just take charge; they also take ownership.

I spent some time talking about stewardship, and as leaders, part of our responsibility is being good stewards over the things which has been entrusted to us. I work in an environment where I am self-governed and interact with others regularly, which means I must manage my time wisely and make the most of the resources entrusted to me. Because the nature of my work can easily invite complacency, maintaining integrity and being a good steward of both my responsibilities and discipline is essential. John Maxwell also writes, "Leadership is a trust, not a right" (Maxwell, 2008, p. 15).

The moment you feel the right to lead can set a negative tone from the start. Leadership is not about entitlement; it is about earning respect and building trust. When someone believes, they are automatically entitled to lead, they risk becoming closed off to feedback, collaboration, and growth. True leadership is grounded in humility, openness, and the ability to foster trust among others.

Trust is the foundation of effective leadership. If followers cannot place their trust in you, they will naturally look elsewhere for guidance, support, or direction. Without trust, leadership loses its influence and connection.

A lack of trust keeps you trapped in a cycle of stagnation. Without trust, you are more likely to fall back into the same patterns and behaviors that caused the setback in the first place. Progress requires vulnerability, openness, and the willingness to trust again, even when it is difficult.

The people we lead must be able to trust us in where we are leading them.

Unfortunately, the children of Israel had a hard time trusting Moses, and it cost them to wander around and not believe God.

When others make excuses, good leaders take responsibility.

We must be accountable in everything we do so that our work will be above reproach. Now, I had said before that no matter what we do as leaders, there will always be people who will just flat out find fault all the time and lie about you every time. I remember we had someone accuse the ministry of taking the money in the back room, so no one could see us taking it. What that person did not understand we had only three people who would do the counting of the offerings, and each person would sign off on what was counted for accountability. The reason was that we did not want everybody in the church knowing everyone's financial business or having money lying out in plain sight. So, I selected trustworthy individuals I could trust to do the counting. I never counted the offerings personally and never wanted to know who gave, so it would not influence me to show favoritism. I only knew the final number, and then we would discuss financial matters at our meetings. I knew the bottom line, let us say. Now, the person tried to accuse us of hiding money; they did not realize also we would send out financial statements at the end of the year, so people could check for themselves their own giving, and because we are a 501c3 ministry and their giving is tax-deductible.

We need to have safeguards that will protect us from false accusations.

In our ministry, we recorded everything said and approved, so we had a record of it. It was a good thing because we had made a financial approval to spend money, putting an addition on the kids' room and extending the office. The amount was large, and one of our elders who was on the board approved of the finances. At the next meeting, when we were going over the financial reports, there was a dent in the bank account because the money was spent on materials and supplies for the additions. The elder was wondering where it went, so we pulled out the minutes from the last meeting and showed him, and reminded him he was part of the approval. The recording of that meeting saved us from any reproach.

The bible also teaches us, "And whatever you do in word or deed, do all in the name of the Lord Jesus, giving thanks to God the Father through Him" (Colossians 3:17). Because God sees everything we do, our actions should be done as unto Him with sincerity, integrity, and purpose. When we live this way, it naturally reflects in how we treat others, becoming a visible testimony of our faith and values. Every decision should be guided by an eternal perspective, one that considers lasting impact beyond the moment. This mindset encourages us to pause, reflect, and reevaluate our choices, ensuring they align with deeper values and purpose rather than fleeting emotions or short-term gains.

Everything we do, we do unto Him because we serve Him, and we want to bring honor to him in all we do. Walking upright and doing what's right is the most important because in the end God sees all things. The scriptures tell us, "And there is no creature hidden from His sight, but all things are naked and open to the eyes of Him to whom we must give account" (Hebrews 4:13).

We must also find those we can trust to keep us accountable and permit them to do so. Too often, however, people think they can rebuke anyone at any time, without permission to do so. It seems like those kinds of folks do not have personal accountability themselves. There are those in my life whom I permitted to speak into my life.

What sets someone apart is their ability to truly understand you, not just through empathy, but through shared experience. They have walked the same path, faced similar struggles, and because of that, you feel safe being open with them. There is no judgment, only acceptance. They recognize your humanity, and that makes all the difference.

We are accountable to others, we are accountable to ourselves, we are accountable to our families, and most importantly, we are accountable to God.

John Maxwell writes, "Effective leadership is the ability to lead yourself before you lead others" (Maxwell, 2008, p 15). If we cannot lead ourselves, there is no way we can lead others. I once heard that if you can master your mind, you can master your world, and that is the essence of self-leadership. It begins with mental discipline: the ability to direct your thoughts, manage your emotions, and stay focused on what truly matters. When you lead yourself well internally, your external world starts to reflect that clarity, purpose, and strength. Mastery of the mind is not just about control; it is about alignment with your values, vision, and goals.

We must master ourselves because if things master us, then we have not mastered anything.

Once we master our lives through self-control, then we can begin to lead. Our first responsibility is our home and family because if we can lead them, we can lead others.

As an overseer, my role extends beyond leadership; it is also a calling to teach and guide. As a teacher, I carry the responsibility to study diligently and grow in understanding so I can rightly divide the Word of truth (II Timothy 2:15) and teach according to Scripture. Yet this responsibility does not end with others; it begins with me. I must remain a lifelong learner, continually seeking wisdom and revelation. As my spiritual leader emphasized in chapter 1: "Stay teachable and you will go far." That posture of humility and openness is what sustains true leadership.

The scriptures teach us, "For we must all appear before the judgment seat of Christ, that each one may receive the things done in the body, according to what he has done, whether good or bad" (II Corinthians 5:10). Remember what I said about keeping things in the light of eternity. Well, this scripture helps reinforce that perspective; we must all appear and give an account of what we have done, whether good or evil. Always keep this scripture in mind when we conduct ourselves, in our ministry life, our business life, and in our everyday life. They used to say that honesty is the best policy, and that is still true today. When we are honest and upfront, we do not have to remember or even follow our tracks. The dishonest person will always have to remember what they did because they will end up slipping. I remember being asked to give a message to one of the graduating classes at our local high school. My message was this: as you leave here today and go into your purpose in life, whether college, starting a business, or even in the local workforce, your character and integrity must always stay intact. I explained to them the difference between the two: character is how we operate when everyone is watching, and integrity is how we operate when no one is watching. The one thing about my wife and me is that what you see in church is what you will see at home. There is no façade in who we are; we live by a standard, we are honest, and we are trustworthy because God is to whom we will answer. Even though we were burned in the past for being trustworthy and honest, we continue to live by that standard.

Jesus told us this, "And I will give you the keys of the kingdom of heaven, and whatever you bind on earth will be bound in heaven, and whatever you loose on earth will be loosed in heaven" (Matthew 16:19). Keys symbolize authority and responsibility. When someone holds the keys, they possess the power to open and close, to grant access or secure boundaries. The verse Matthew 16:19 highlights the weight of spiritual authority; those entrusted with it must steward it wisely, knowing their actions carry eternal significance.

Keys are given to those who normally have responsibility, and Jesus has given us the keys because He trusts us with the responsibility to use those keys. We are accountable for using these keys accordingly. The meaning of keys in this passage is "kleis," which means the power to open and shut. In the New Testament, it denotes power and authority of various kinds" (BlueletterBible, 2021). The word keys is plural, so many keys have been given to us for opening and shutting. These keys can open the healing realms of the Kingdom, open the financial realm of the Kingdom, and open the jewels of wisdom of the Kingdom. The keys can also open the doors to other people's destinies. That is a great responsibility in and of itself, and we must use those keys with great responsibility. The keys can shut up the powers of hell, shut up sickness, and can close and lock the doors to our past. Keys are normally given to those who are trustworthy and reliable, and Christ has given them to us, His church.

God often begins by entrusting us with small responsibilities to test our character, discipline, and faithfulness. It is in these seemingly minor tasks that our accountability and trustworthiness are revealed. When we consistently show integrity by doing what is right, even when no one is watching, and take ownership of our actions, we demonstrate that we can be trusted with more. Spiritual authority is not given lightly. It is cultivated through obedience, humility, and a proven track record of stewardship. Luke 16:10 says, "Whoever can be trusted with very little can also be trusted with much…" This principle reflects how God evaluates our readiness. If we are faithful in the small, He knows we will be faithful in the greater.

Practical Application

- Think of a recent decision you made as a leader. How did accountability (to God, others, or yourself) influence that decision?
- What new accountability practices could you implement this week in your leadership, ministry, or personal life?
- The author shared an example of safeguards put in place around church finances. What safeguards do you currently

have (or need to implement) in your leadership role to protect from false accusations or misconduct?

- How can transparency and record-keeping strengthen accountability in both ministry and business?

Chapter 7
Tale of Two Kings

Pride

The scriptures teach us, "Pride goes before destruction, And a haughty spirit before a fall" (Proverbs 16:18). If we do not turn from our pride, the fall will come, and yet God gives us grace to change. There are two accounts in the Bible in which I call the tales of two kings. The first is found in II Chronicles 26 about a king named Uzziah. He was sixteen years old when he was made king, and he reigned for fifty-two years in Jerusalem. The scriptures tell us he did what was right in the eyes of the Lord and did amazing things.

Uzziah was a successful king of Judah. He expanded the kingdom, fortified Jerusalem, and led military victories. His fame spread far and wide. With such accomplishments, he may have begun to see himself as above reproach even in spiritual matters. Pride often blinds people to correction. When the priests confronted him, Uzziah became angry rather than repentant. This reaction shows how pride can harden the heart, making it resistant to truth even when it's delivered by spiritual authorities.

Pride can quietly take root in a leader's heart when success becomes a constant companion. With each achievement, recognition, or promotion, it's easy to start believing that one's own abilities are solely responsible for the outcomes. This mindset can shift a leader from gratitude to entitlement, making them less receptive to feedback and more likely to dismiss the contributions of others. Over time, the humility that once grounded your leadership may erode, replaced by a subtle sense of superiority that blinds them to their own limitations.

Until one day pride filled his heart, and this is the rest of the account: when his pride filled his heart:

But when he was strong, his heart was lifted, to his destruction, for he transgressed against the Lord his God by entering the temple of the Lord to burn incense on the altar of incense. So Azariah the priest went in after him, and with him were eighty priests of the Lord—valiant men. And they withstood King Uzziah, and said to him, it is not for you, Uzziah, to burn incense to the Lord, but for the priests, the sons of Aaron, who are consecrated to burn incense. Get out of the sanctuary, for you have trespassed! You shall have no honor from the Lord God. Then Uzziah became furious, and he had a censer in his hand to burn incense. And while he was angry with the priests, leprosy broke out on his forehead, before the priests in the house of the Lord, beside the incense altar. And Azariah, the chief priest, and all the priests looked at him, and there, on his forehead, he was leprous; so, they thrust him out of that place. Indeed, he also hurried to get out because the Lord had struck him. King Uzziah was a leper until the day of his death. He dwelt in an isolated house, because he was a leper; for he was cut off from the house of the Lord… (II Chronicles 26:16-21).

His pride caused him to think he could do whatever he wanted; the result was that he was stricken with leprosy and taken out of the presence of the Lord.

Uzziah's success made him feel invincible, leading him to overstep even divine boundaries. The priesthood was for Aaron's descendants (2 Chronicles 26:16–21).

One subtle warning sign that pride or ego may be easing God out is when we stop listening to both others and to God. In leadership or ministry, this can look like dismissing wise counsel, ignoring correction, or relying solely on our own judgment. When prayer becomes an afterthought and feedback feels like a threat, it's often a sign that we've begun to trust ourselves more than the One who called us. This quiet shift can lead us away from humility and into isolation, where ego thrives and God's voice fades. We also dismiss others with authority. The result was that Uzziah was ushered out of the presence of God. The scripture teaches us that God resists the proud but gives grace to the humble (James 4:6).

Which brings me to another King found in the bible named Manasseh. He was twelve years old when he became king and reigned fifty-five years, but he did evil in the sight of the Lord (II Chronicles 33:1-2). He would cause Judah and its inhabitants to do more evil than the other nations (II Chronicles 33:9). The Lord would speak to the people, but they would not listen. The Lord would eventually bring the army of the king of Assyria, who would capture Manasseh and take him away bound to Babylon (II Chronicles 33:10-11). It goes on to say that while in his affliction, he humbled himself greatly before the God of his fathers, and he prayed to God. The result was this: God heard him, "Received his entreaty, heard his supplication, and brought him back to Jerusalem into his kingdom. Then Manasseh knew that the Lord was God" (II Chronicles 33:13).

Not only did God forgive him, but He restored Manasseh to his throne. Back in Jerusalem, Manasseh removed the foreign gods, repaired the altar of the Lord, and urged the people to worship and serve God (2 Chronicles 33:12–16). God doesn't just clean the slate, He rebuilds the life.

Because of his repentance, prayer, and humility, God restored not only Manasseh to the throne but also restored fellowship with God.

Leaders must be willing to own their mistakes without deflecting blame or making excuses. Just as Manasseh humbled himself before God, effective restoration requires a sincere heart that seeks forgiveness and actively works to make things right. This might mean initiating difficult conversations, rebuilding trust through consistent actions, and showing genuine remorse. When leaders lead with repentance, they create space for grace, reconciliation, and renewed unity.

Good leaders are transparent about their shortcomings and quick to seek forgiveness when they have caused harm. Publicly, this might mean acknowledging mistakes in front of a team or congregation, showing that leadership isn't about perfection but integrity. Privately, it involves honest self-reflection, accountability, and a willingness to be corrected. When leaders consistently demonstrate humility by listening well, serving, and placing God's will above their own, they create a culture where grace and growth thrive.

My wife Lynette always said, "It's not how you start the race, but how you finish that is what's important."

Staying grounded in purpose, guarding against pride, and finishing strong requires intentional rhythms that keep your heart aligned with God and your leadership rooted in love. Sometimes, it is not how we start the race but how we finish that is important.

These two different accounts of these two kings can really speak to us, even as leaders, about how pride and arrogance can lead to our downfall. However, when we stay in a place of humility and are honest when we make mistakes, we will always walk with the grace of God in our lives. One thing I have noticed in ministry and being in a leadership position is that people love honesty, and when they see a leader being honest and owning up when making a mistake, they appreciate you, respect you, and even want to follow you that much more. Too often, we want to create an image that we do not make mistakes, and when we do, we try to make excuses that become a turn-off to those around us. Remember what David did when confronted with his sin: he owned up to it and repented. See Psalm 51.

Reflection Questions

- Think of a time you allowed pride to affect your decision-making. What did you learn from that experience?
- What steps can you take to maintain a "soft heart" before God and others in positions of leadership or influence?
- In what ways can you cultivate a habit of prayer and repentance to keep pride in check?

Conclusion

In conclusion, let us take time to reflect on who we are as leaders. What kind of leader are you? Many resources explore the different styles and approaches to leadership, each offering valuable insight. I hope that through this book and its teaching and my personal experiences, you have taken something, perhaps just one key insight that will help you grow and flourish in your leadership journey. Leadership is about influence, service, and the legacy we leave in the lives of others. I encourage you to pause, pray, and ask the Lord to reveal areas where you need help in shaping you into the leader He has called you to be.

References

- BlueletterBible, (2021). https://www.blueletterbible.org/
- Evans, D. (2020). The Spirit of Absalom by Dee Evans (hiskingdomprophecy.com).
- Maxwell, J. (2008). The leadership Handbook: 26 Critical lessons Every Leader Needs. Orange, California: Yates &Yates Publishing
- Merriam-Webster. (1828). https://www.merriam-webster.com/.
- New American Standard Bible (1977,1995, 2020).
- https://www.biblegateway.com/versions/New-American-Standard-Bible-NASB
- New King James Version, The Holy Bible. (1982, 2013). Nashville, TN: Thomas Nelson Publishing
- New Living Translation, The Holy Bible. (1996, 2004, 2015). Tyndale House Foundation

Made in the USA
Las Vegas, NV
03 December 2025

35651948R00039